THE WITCH'S DOG AND THE BOX OF TRICKS

Frank Rodgers has written and illustrated a wide range of books for children: picture books, storybooks, non-fiction and novels. His children's stories have been broadcast on radio and TV and a sitcom series was created for CBBC based on his book *The Intergalactic Kitchen*. His recent work for Puffin includes the Eyetooth books and the bestselling Witch's Dog, and Robodog titles. He was an art teacher before becoming an author and illustrator and lives in Glasgow with his wife. He has two grown-up children.

FRANK RODGERS

The **Witch's Dog**
and the
Box of Tricks

PUFFIN

For Will

PUFFIN BOOKS

Published by the Penguin Group
Penguin Books Ltd, 80 Strand, London WC2R 0RL, England
Penguin Group (USA) Inc., 375 Hudson Street, New York, New York 10014, USA
Penguin Group (Canada), 10 Alcorn Avenue, Toronto, Ontario,
Canada M4V 3B2 (a division of Pearson Penguin Canada Inc.)
Penguin Ireland, 25 St Stephen's Green, Dublin 2, Ireland (a division of Penguin Books Ltd)
Penguin Group (Australia), 250 Camberwell Road, Camberwell,
Victoria 3124, Australia (a division of Pearson Australia Group Pty Ltd)
Penguin Books India Pvt Ltd, 11 Community Centre,
Panchsheel Park, New Delhi – 110 017, India Penguin Group (NZ),
cnr Airborne and Rosedale Roads, Albany, Auckland 1310,
New Zealand (a division of Pearson New Zealand Ltd)
Penguin Books (South Africa) (Pty) Ltd, 24 Sturdee Avenue, Rosebank,
Johannesburg 2196, South Africa

Penguin Books Ltd, Registered Offices: 80 Strand, London WC2R 0RL, England

www.penguin.com

First published 2005
1

Copyright © Frank Rodgers, 2005
All rights reserved

The moral right of the author/illustrator has been asserted

Typeset in Times New Roman Infant
Printed in China by Midas Printing Ltd

British Library Cataloguing in Publication Data
A CIP catalogue record for this book is available from the British Library

ISBN 0–141–31813–9

Wilf the witch's dog was in the
kitchen practising for his
school concert. He was blowing his
trumpet very softly as he didn't
want Weenie to hear the tune he
was playing.

Just to make sure,
he had also
stuffed a sock
inside the trumpet.

In the next room, Weenie was busy
writing out the concert programme.

She was the
organizer
and wanted
everything
to run
smoothly.

Weenie glanced at the clock. "Good," she said, smiling. "I've got plenty of time before the concert begins. No need to hurry."

A sudden knock at the front door made her look round.

"I'll get it, Weenie," called Wilf, coming in and hurrying to the front door.

A moment later he came back in with a big smile on his face . . .

and a big parcel in his paws.

"It was the postman
with a special delivery,
Weenie," he said
gleefully.

"I ordered it from the shop. It's for
you. Happy birthday!"

Weenie laughed in delight as Wilf
gave her the parcel.
"Thank you, Wilf," she cried. "What
a surprise. I'd quite forgotten it was
my birthday today."

Excitedly Weenie opened the parcel.

"What a nice box,"
she exclaimed. "Red
with gold stars."

"I hope you like what's inside,"
said Wilf.
Weenie opened the box and blinked,
puzzled.
"But there's nothing
inside the box,
Wilf," she said.
"It's empty."

"What?" cried Wilf. He peered into the box too and gasped. "So it is.

They must've forgotten to put the present in at the shop."

"What a shame, Wilf," said Weenie sadly. "Your nice surprise spoiled."

Wilf sighed but then smiled. "Never mind," he said. "I'll take the box with me to the school concert and go to the shop directly afterwards. You'll get your present later."

"That will be just as good, Wilf," replied Weenie, beaming.

At that moment Wilf saw his friends
coming into the garden.
"Harry, Bertie and
Streaky have got their
musical instruments with
them," he said.

"It must be time to go to the
concert."

Weenie gasped and
whirled round.
"It can't be! I'm the
organizer. I have
to be there first. I
thought I had
plenty of time."

She picked up the clock and groaned.
"I might have known. It's stopped.
This old clock
is always doing
that. Now I'm
late!"

Hastily she grabbed the concert
programme and hurried out of the
door. "See you later, Wilf."

In the yard she jumped on to her
broomstick and quickly
shot into
the air . . .

zooming over the heads of Harry,
Bertie and Streaky as they propped
their instrument cases against the
wall.

"There goes Weenie,"
chuckled Bertie. "In
a hurry as usual."

As they walked into the kitchen
Bertie winked at Wilf and pointed to
the trumpet.

"Did you practise the
special tune, Wilf?"
he asked.

Wilf grinned as he pulled the sock
out of his trumpet. "I did," he
replied.
"So did we," said
Harry. "It's going to
be a nice surprise for
you-know-who."

"Come on, Wilf," Streaky cried,
eager to be off.

"Let's go or
we'll be late
too."

Wilf put his trumpet into the box
and smiled. "I have to take this box
with me," he said. "It makes a great
trumpet case, doesn't it?"

In the school hall nearly every seat was taken as witches and their pets waited for the concert to begin. Everyone was excited.

But, at the side of the stage, Weenie was fretting as she checked her list.

"Oh, dear," she said. "The dancer, the juggler and the acrobat are here but the conjurer hasn't turned up.

I wonder where he is? The concert starts in a few minutes!"

Backstage, Sly Cat and Tricky Toad sat with their feet up. They were supposed to be helping with the scenery but they were too lazy.

"Concerts are silly," muttered Sly.

"Yeah, silly," agreed Tricky.

When Wilf and his friends came in,
Sly and Tricky sat up and scowled.
They had always been jealous
of Wilf.

"What's in the box, Wilf?" asked Sly
with a sneer.

"My trumpet,"
Wilf replied.

Sly sniggered. "Can't wait to hear what kind of silly music you're going to play," he said. "I bet you'll be rotten."

"Yeah, rotten," repeated Tricky.

Bertie glowered. "We're going to be good," he retorted.

"Of course we are,"
added Wilf airily,
turning away.
"You'll see."

"Maybe they will
be good," whispered Tricky
jealously. Sly's eyes narrowed.

"Well, we'll just have to find a way
to make sure they're not, won't we?"
he hissed sneakily.

Suddenly the door flew open and
Weenie rushed in.

"Wilf!" she cried. "There's a
problem! The conjurer hasn't arrived
and he's due on stage soon.
Do you think you could
go and look for him?

He might have lost
his way. You and
your friends are last
on the programme
so you've got time to
do it."

"Of course," Wilf replied quickly.

"We'll help!" cried Harry,
Bertie and Streaky, hurrying
after Wilf and Weenie
as they ran out
of the door.

When they were left alone, Sly
grinned wickedly.
"Now's our chance," he said, taking
Wilf's trumpet out of the box. "We'll
make sure Wilf can't play in the
concert by hiding this!"

"Brilliant!" cried Tricky,
slapping the box in
delight.

Immediately the lid of the box sprang open and a cascade of brightly coloured streamers and flags burst out.

Sly and Tricky jumped in alarm . . . but then Sly slowly smiled.

"Aha!" he crowed. "I recognize that box now! It belongs to the conjurer."

Sly winked at Tricky. "I don't know how Wilf got the box but I've just had a great idea. It'll spoil the concert for Wilf . . . *and* for the conjurer."

"What's the idea?" asked Tricky excitedly.

26

"We'll cast a super-glue spell on everything," answered Sly gleefully. "That way the instruments will stick inside their cases and the trumpet will be jammed up with the box's tricks. Hah, hah!"

"Hah, hah!" echoed Tricky. "Let's do it!"

Outside, Wilf and his friends were
searching for the conjurer. As they
came round a corner they saw
someone not far off.

"That's him!"
exclaimed Harry.
"And he's going the
wrong way! Come on,
let's catch
him up."

Wilf and the others ran after the
conjurer and stopped him.

"You'll have to hurry," said Wilf
after he and his friends explained
who they were. "You're due on
stage soon."

"I'm sorry to be late," replied the conjurer. "I had to pick up some things from the shop and then I lost my way."

Bertie hefted the conjurer's heavy bag on to his shoulders as if it weighed nothing.

"Let's get back as fast as we can," he said briskly.

Weenie was overjoyed
to see the conjurer.

"Just in time!" she
exclaimed. "You're
on next."

"Righty-ho," replied the conjurer.
Quickly he took his bag from Bertie . . .

and trotted on to the stage to a big
round of applause.

"Hello, everyone," he called, "and welcome to *Conjuring Time*! In my bag I have some very interesting things . . . including a perfectly ordinary, empty box.

But, as you will soon see, it's an empty box that's *full of tricks*."

Rummaging in his bag he brought
out a box.

"Here we are," he
declared proudly,
"My box
of . . ."

Suddenly he stopped and peered at
the box.
"This isn't it," he said.
"My box of tricks is red
with gold stars. This
box is gold with
red stars."

Watching from the wings, Wilf
gasped.
"*That's* the box with Weenie's
present in it!" he
cried.

There's been a
mix-up at the shop.
The conjurer's box
is in the dressing
room with my
trumpet in it."

Wilf dashed off, followed by Harry,
Bertie and Streaky.

They ran into the dressing room just
as Sly and Tricky finished their spell.

"Come for your instruments, everyone?" asked Sly innocently.

Bertie looked at him suspiciously.

"Yes," replied Wilf. "But first I have to give back this box to the conjurer."

He opened the box and quickly took
out the trumpet.
Sly and Tricky stared at each other
in disbelief.
"How . . .?" gasped
Tricky.

"Our super-glue spell didn't work,"
hissed Sly angrily.

But just as Harry,
Bertie and
Streaky
opened their
instrument
cases . . .

the trumpet gave a loud TOOT all
on its own.
Wilf got such a
fright that he
dropped it.

Then everyone watched in
amazement as the trumpet tooted
again and began to bounce round
the room like a pogo-stick.

Quick as a flash the double bass, guitar and drums hopped out of their cases and bounded after the trumpet.

The instruments thumped across the floor making a noise like an entire orchestra falling downstairs . . .

the double bass booming, the trumpet blaring, the guitar twanging and the drums banging.

The din was terrible. The bouncing
musical instruments knocked over
chairs and bits of scenery . . .

and Sly and Tricky leapt into
Bertie's big case for safety.

Suddenly the instruments bolted out
of the door and on to the stage.

"Stop them!" cried
Wilf.

Harry, Bertie, Streaky and Wilf
raced in pursuit.

Speedy Streaky quickly caught up
with one of his drums . . .

but it slipped out of his paws.
Harry and Wilf tried hard to catch
the guitar and the trumpet . . .

but the instruments always seemed
to be one jump ahead.

Then Bertie, with a huge leap,
landed on his double bass and held
on tightly.

"Whoa!" he cried, but it was no use.
The double bass bounced all over

the stage . . .
its big bottom
banging down
loudly on the
boards.

In dismay, Wilf saw it was about to
bounce on to the box that held
Weenie's present.

Frantically he sent out a rescue spell.

The sparkling spell
flashed around the box
just as the double
bass came down . . .

CRUNCH!
and flattened it.

"Oh, no!" wailed Wilf.
"That was your
present, Weenie."

"Such a shame, Wilf," cried Weenie
above the noise. "But never mind.

Let's use magic
to sort all of
this out!"

Quickly Wilf aimed spells at his
trumpet and Bertie's double bass.

Weenie did the same with Harry's
guitar and Streaky's drums.

The four spells crackled out and . . .

FLASH!

In an instant the instruments were
back to normal.

Everyone cheered as the wild chase
and the awful din ended.

"Well done, Weenie and Wilf,"
exclaimed the
head teacher.
"You've saved
the concert from
disaster." She
looked about
her, confused.
"But who
caused it all?"

Bertie growled.
"I've got a very
good idea it was
Sly and Tricky,"
he said.

49

Backstage, Sly and Tricky were still
in Bertie's big case, even though its
lid was open.

"Come out of
there!" demanded
the head teacher.

"We can't," whined Sly. "We're
stuck."
"Yeah, stuck," echoed Tricky.

The head teacher slowly smiled and nodded. "I understand," she said. "It seems that *someone* tried a super-glue spell and got it all wrong." She looked at Sly and Tricky sternly.

"So the *two someones* will just have to stay where they are until the concert is over."

Wilf gave the box back to the
delighted conjurer.
"At least your box
is all right," he
said with a sigh.

"Thank you, Wilf," replied the
conjurer, quickly inspecting it.

"It does look all right. But I'd better
try it out to see if it still works."
He tapped twice on the lid.

Immediately out sprang a
jack-in-the-box . . .

with a clock in its hands.

"What's this clock doing in my box?" asked the surprised conjurer.

Wilf gasped in astonishment.
"It's Weenie's present!" he cried.
"My rescue
spell worked
after all.

It transported the clock into the
conjurer's box just before my box
was smashed."

"Oh, Wilf," said Weenie. "It's just
what I need. I'll never be late again.
What a lovely surprise."

Wilf grinned.
"There's one more
surprise to come,
Weenie," he said.

Harry, Bertie and Streaky gathered
round with their instruments at the
ready.

"One, two, three," Wilf counted
and the little band began to play
the tune they had been practising
in secret.

"*Happy birthday to you . . .*"
The audience clapped and cheered
and began to sing along to the band.

"*Happy birthday, dear Weenie.
Happy birthday to you! Hip-hip,
hooray!*"

"You're a genius, Wilf," said Weenie when they had finished. "It's my best birthday ever."

"It certainly was full of surprises," replied Wilf.

"And here's another one," Weenie went on with a giggle. "Just for you."

From behind the curtain she produced a gold box covered in red stars.

"I used a repairing spell on the broken box," she explained.

"It's as good as new . . . and perfect to keep your trumpet in."

Wilf laughed in delight.

"Thanks, Weenie," he said. "And just so there are no more surprises, I'm going to write on it . . .

THIS IS WILF'S TRUMPET CASE...

DEFINITELY NOT
A BOX OF TRICKS!